# MISSION ALERT
## LAB 101

# BENJAMIN HULME-CROSS

Illustrated by
## Kanako and Yuzuru

BLOOMSBURY EDUCATION
AN IMPRINT OF BLOOMSBURY

LONDON OXFORD NEW

Tom and his twin sister Zilla go to a boarding
school. They don't like it very much. But Tom
and Zilla have a secret. They work as spies
for the Secret Service. Sometimes there is a
spy mission that children are better at than
grown-ups. That's when Tom and Zilla get their
next Mission Alert!

# CONTENTS

Chapter One                              7

Chapter Two                          18

Chapter Three                    31

Chapter Four                      46

# Chapter One

Tom and Zilla sat at their computers. Their homework was coding, and Tom was working hard.

"You're so slow at coding," laughed Zilla. Tom didn't answer. He wanted to finish the line of code he was writing. Then, suddenly the screen went blank and they both groaned.

Sometimes the school computers shut down without warning. It was very annoying!

Then their watches started buzzing, and a message flashed up on each of their watch screens. MISSION ALERT!

Zilla and Tom plugged earphones into their watches. The watches had lots of special spy features. The Secret Service could find Zilla and Tom at any time by tracking their watches. They tapped the screens and the instructions began.

"Agents, here is your next mission," they heard Marcus say. Marcus was their handler at the Secret Service. "It will take place as part of a school trip."

Tom and Zilla looked at each other. They didn't think it would be easy to keep their mission secret if they were surrounded by people who knew them. Missions that took them away from school were much better!

"As you know, there is a school trip to a robotics centre this week," said Marcus.

This was true. Everyone in their year at school was excited about the trip. Someone said that remote control robot battles were held at the centre.

"We set up this whole trip just to get you two inside the robotics centre," said Marcus. "The centre is owned by a company which has links with dangerous criminal gangs. Last month one of our spies hacked in to the robotics centre's systems and found plans to build a huge number of robots. We think they are planning to hire them out to the gangs."

"Why would the criminal gangs want to do that?" asked Zilla.

"That's what we want you to find out," said Marcus. "The emails talked about 'Lab 101' which is somewhere inside the robotics centre. Your mission is to find Lab 101 and find out what is going on."

"But why can't you just close the place down, or break in and arrest everyone?" Tom asked.

"We've been watching the centre for weeks now, and the only people who go in or out are groups of children on school trips," said Marcus. "We haven't seen any adults enter or leave the building. We need more information before we go in."

Then Marcus showed them some maps and floorplans of the robotics centre. He told Tom and Zilla to study the maps so they would know where everything was inside the centre and how to find Lab 101.

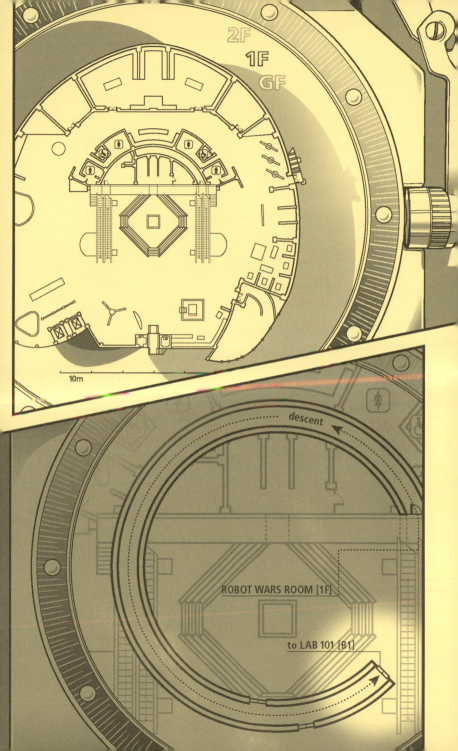

2F
1F
GF

10m

descent

ROBOT WARS ROOM [1F]

to LAB 101 [B1]

# Chapter 2

The day of the school trip arrived. All the children were very excited. Their teacher, Mr Stevens, was not allowed to go into the centre.

It was just for children. So Mr Stevens stayed in the entrance area. A tour guide dressed in purple led the children over towards a short tunnel. "That guide has got very bright blue eyes," thought Zilla.

"To get into the robotics centre we have to go through this scanner one at a time," said the guide. "We scan everyone who comes here so that we get better and better at creating robots who can move like humans."

One by one, the children went through the tunnel, standing on a very slow conveyer belt. Zilla was last. When it was her turn, the guide held open the gate and she stepped onto the conveyor belt. On the way through it was like being inside a computer.

She heard a very high-pitched noise all around her. Very bright lights spun around her as she passed through. It felt really strange and Zilla was glad to get to the other side.

When she got out of the scanner, Zilla
saw a huge sign hanging from the ceiling.
ROBOT WARS ROOM. A group of children was
standing around Tom. Zilla saw that Tom had a
remote control in his hands. He was controlling

a robot that was zooming around in a pit in front of him. A few people dressed like the tour guide were trying to fix the robots that had got broken when they crashed into each other. There were bits of metal everywhere.

Tom seemed to be having fun. "I bet he's forgotten why we are here," thought Zilla.

She looked around the large room they were in. In each corner was a CCTV camera. All four of them seemed to be pointing at Tom and the other children. The tour guide was standing near the tunnel they had come through. He was just staring straight ahead with his strange blue eyes.

Over on the other side of the room Zilla saw more people dressed in purple. She wondered if they had strange eyes too. She walked over towards them. Sure enough, they had the same blue eyes that were a bit too bright.

Then one of the people suddenly opened a door and left the room. Zilla saw that to open the door he used an ID card which was hanging on his belt. It gave her an idea.

She went back to the robot pit in the middle of the room, looking for a sharp bit of metal.

She saw what she needed and picked it up. Then she walked over to the tour guide and stood next to him. Very carefully, she reached out a hand and found his ID card. With the piece of metal she cut the string and then she slipped the card in her pocket.

"Time to find out what's going on in Lab 101," she thought.

# Chapter 3

As soon as the door hissed closed behind her, Zilla felt better. There was something not quite right about the tour guide and his friends and it was good to get away from them.

She remembered the map from Marcus's instructions, and she set off along the white corridors of the robotics centre. In less than two minutes she was standing outside a door with a sign that read, 'Lab 101'.

There were no windows into the lab and Zilla had no idea what she would find inside. She took a deep breath, waved her tour guide's ID card over the scanner next to the doorway, and went in. She left her coat on the floor to stop the door closing behind her and looked around.

The room was completely white. The only things in the room were three computers lined up on a long table in the middle. She walked across to the computers.

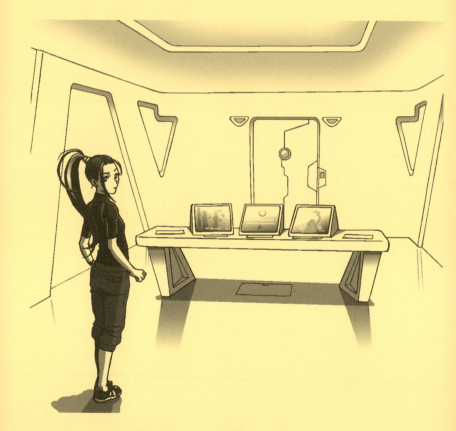

A progress bar took up most of the central screen. Under the progress bar were the words:

DO NOT ADJUST UNTIL PRINTING IS COMPLETE.

The screen on the left showed live footage of her friends, still looking down into the robot pit. There were three children with remote controls now, and three robots crashing into each other on the ground. She could not see Tom anywhere.

"Maybe he's on his way," Zilla thought, looking at the third screen. This screen showed an image of Zilla herself in the scanning tunnel on the way into the centre. The image was a close-up of her face. A grid of bright green lines was shining on her skin in the picture. "Scary," she thought.

"I'm going to find out what they are printing and then get out of here," Zilla said to herself.

At the back of the room was another door. It had a small window in it. What she saw through the window gave her the biggest shock of her life.

A huge machine was building something. The machine was like a giant arm. It looked like the sort of thing you might find in a car factory. And it seemed to be building a human being.

The human figure that the machine was building wore purple clothes. It was almost complete. The only thing missing was the head. Where the head should have been, Zilla could see lights and wires. Just then, the machine's arm twisted up and over the purple figure, and brought a head down to rest on its shoulders.

"It's 3D printing a robot!" Zilla thought.

Then Zilla looked at the head. Her heart nearly stopped. Looking back at her, through bright blue eyes, was her own face!

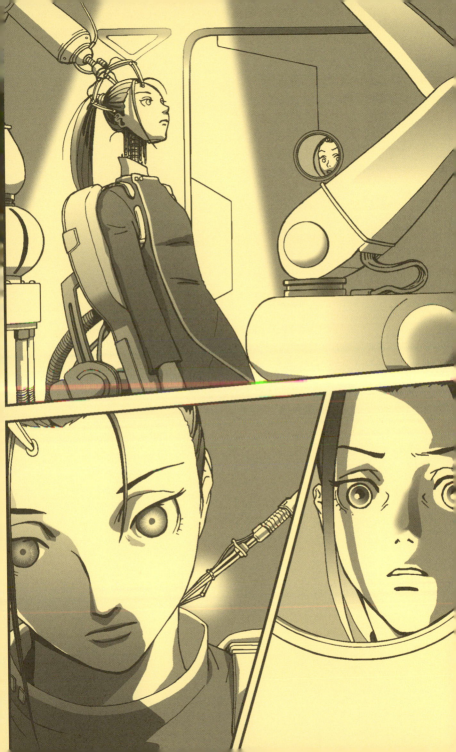

She watched as the robot Zilla was switched on. Robot Zilla looked around the printing room, then turned and left through a door at the back of the room.

"So they are making robot doubles of me and my friends!" thought Zilla. Her fear was mixed with anger. She waved the ID pass over the scanner, walked through the printing room and followed Robot Zilla through the final door.

# Chapter 4

Just as Zilla walked through the final door,
Tom entered the room with the computers in
it. He had no ID card, but he had followed one
of the people wearing purple out of the robot
wars room.

When he got to Lab 101 he found the door held open by Zilla's coat.

Tom walked over to the computers, just like Zilla had done before him. The middle screen now showed:

EDIT SINGLE ROBOT SETTINGS OR

SELECT ALL.

Tom scratched his head and looked at the other screens. One still showed the robot wars room. The other showed line upon line of purple-clothed figures. They were all standing very still, apart from one who was walking towards the back of the group.

With a gasp, Tom saw that it was Zilla. At least, he thought it was Zilla. A moment later he saw Zilla following Zilla. There were two of them! One had purple clothes on, and one had Zilla's normal clothes on.

"Of course!" he realised. "That's why they scanned us! They are making 3D copies to clone us!"

Just as this thought flashed through Tom's mind, he saw that the rest of the purple robots had begun to move. All together, they were walking towards the real Zilla. They had blocked off her path back to the door.

He could see that she was screaming, and he ran to the door of the printing room. But he had no ID card, so he could not open it. He ran back to the computers.

EDIT SINGLE ROBOT SETTINGS OR SELECT ALL.

Tom clicked "SELECT ALL" and hoped that he could find some way of stopping the robots.

He looked at the options:

LANGUAGE SETTINGS

WEAPONS SETTINGS

SLEEP SETTINGS.

Next Tom clicked SLEEP SETTINGS.

He looked again at the screen showing Zilla and the robots. They had made a wide circle around her now. She was trying to push her way through them and they were stopping her.

On the screen Tom saw that SLEEP WHEN HUMANS ARE PRESENT was one of the options. Tom selected it and hit ENTER. A loading wheel appeared on the screen.

The circle of robots around Zilla was getting closer and closer to her. She tried to push them away but they were much too strong for her.

Tom noticed their bright blue eyes. It was the clue he needed to work out what was going on. "The whole place is being run by robots!" he thought. "That's why Marcus said they didn't see any members of staff entering or leaving the building." On the screen Tom could see Zilla trapped in a circle of robots.

Then, the loading wheel on Tom's screen disappeared and, at once, all the robots stopped moving and closed their eyes.

Zilla gave one of the robots a push. It fell over, knocking all the other robots over like a line of dominoes.

Zilla ran to the door, through the printing room and back into Lab 101. She gave a cry when she saw Tom.

"It's OK," said Tom. "I've put them to sleep."

"Look at this," said Zilla. She had found a folder behind one of the computers. It had lots of pictures of robots with human faces.

"So that's why they scanned us on the way in," said Tom. "Each robot is a copy of a real person. If you're going to break the law you hire one of the robots to do it for you. Then if there are witnesses, the person who the robot was copied from gets the blame instead of you."

"I think we've found out what goes on in Lab 101," said Zilla. "Let's get out of here and report back to Marcus."

# Bonus Bits!

## ABOUT THE AUTHOR

Here are some interesting facts about Benjamin Hulme-Cross:

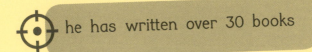 he has written over 30 books

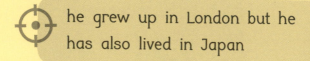 he grew up in London but he has also lived in Japan

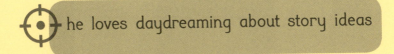 he loves daydreaming about story ideas

## QUIZ TIME?

Why not test your knowledge of the story by trying these multiple choice questions. Look back at the story if you need to. There are answers at the end (no peeking!).

1. What was Tom working on when the 'Mission Alert' came in?

A  maths

B  history

C  reading

D  coding

2. What did Zilla and Tom have to plug into their watches to find out about the mission?

A  earphones

B  mini tv sets

C  phones

D  microphones

3. Who had planned the school trip to the robotics centre?

A     the class teacher

B     the head teacher

C     the Secret Service

D     Lab 101

4. Why did Zilla take a sharp bit of metal from the robot pit?

A     to harm the guide

B     to cut the string on the guide's ID card

C     to open a door

D     to write a message on glass

5.  What did Zilla use to stop the door closing behind her?

A     her bag

B     the metal she had taken

C     her coat

D     her shoes

6.  What gave Zilla the 'biggest shock of her life'?

A     the size of the building

B     Tom being held prisoner

C     all the robots

D     the 3D printer printing a human

# WHAT NEXT?

If you enjoyed reading this story and haven't already read Greyfields, grab yourself a copy and curl up somewhere to read it!

Do you think you would like to be a spy like Tom and Zilla? Why not write a story about yourself being a spy and solving a case. What gadgets you would use? What villain would you have to defeat?

ANSWERS to QUIZ TIME?

1D, 2A, 3C, 4B, 5C, 6D,

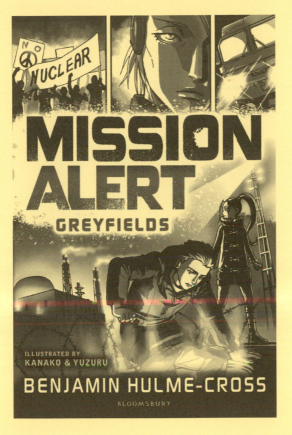

Tom and Zilla are back with a new secret spy mission. They must save the Greyfields nuclear power plant from a sinister plot. One thing's for sure: if Greyfields isn't safe, no one is...

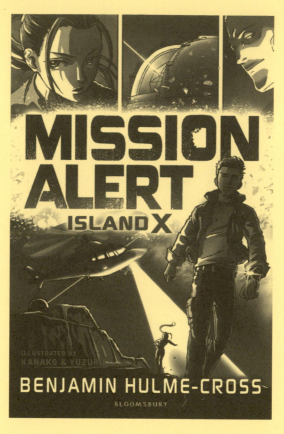

Join agents Tom and Zilla on another
top-secret spy mission: to investigate an evil
billionaire and a mysterious island.
On Island X, danger is never far away...

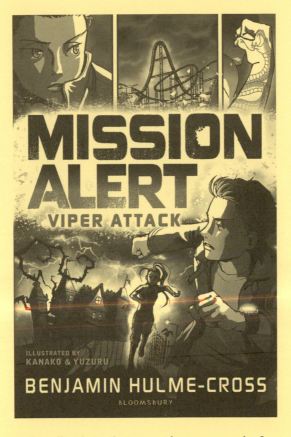

Tom and Zilla head to a theme park for their latest secret spy mission: protecting the son of a famous scientist from the evil Viper gang. You never know when the Vipers will attack!

For more high low fiction from Bloomsbury
Education visit www.bloomsbury.com